Witty Minister Stories

ADAPTED FROM THE ORIGINAL AMAR CHITRA KATHA COMICS!

First published in India in 2023 by HarperCollins Children's Books
An imprint of HarperCollins Publishers
4th Floor, Tower A, Building No. 10, Phase II, DLF Cyber City,
Gurugram, Haryana – 122002
www.harpercollins.co.in

6 8 10 9 7 5

Text © Amar Chitra Katha 2023
Illustrations © Amar Chitra Katha 2023

P-ISBN: 978-935-6990-05-0
E-ISBN: 978-935-6990-07-4

This is a work of fiction and all characters and incidents described in this book are the product of the author's imagination. Any resemblance to actual persons, living or dead, is entirely coincidental.

Neel Debdutt Paul asserts the moral right to be identified as the author of this work.

All rights reserved. No part of this publication may be reproduced, stored in a retrieval system, or transmitted, in any form or by any means, electronic, mechanical, photocopying, recording or otherwise, without the prior permission of the publishers.

Cover and inside illustrations: Based on the artwork in the original Amar Chitra Katha comics

Typeset in Baloo 13pt/ 16
by Ketan Tondwalkar

Printed and bound at Nutech Print Services - India

This book is printed on FSC® certified paper
which ensures responsible forest management.

WITTY MINISTER STORIES

Adapted from the original
Amar Chitra Katha comics

WRITTEN BY
NEEL DEBDUTT PAUL

contents

How Akbar Met Birbal	7
Tenali Raman Foils the Thieves	22
Gopal in the Sweet Shop	40
The Corrupt Official	53
Tenali and the Horse's Mouth	68
Gopal and the Petty Thief	94
The Wise Answer	112

HOW AKBAR MET BIRBAL

Though the great Mughal emperor, Akbar, was born into a powerful dynasty of rulers, he was a man of the people. Nothing gave him more joy than to dress up as a commoner and roam the streets of Agra. It was his favourite thing to do and he did it often.

At this time in history, Agra was bustling with activity. It was the capital of the Mughal empire. It was also the heart of the country, with thousands of people coming in and out – trading, selling and making a living.

Emperor Akbar had always encouraged culture. He had encouraged bookbinders and writers, rishis and imams, scholars and teachers, all to flock to the city. Learning thrived. Performers and entertainers also flocked to the city. Musicians like Tansen had blossomed in Akbar's court. Hundreds of theatre groups and behrupiya (impressionists) troupes had also been drawn to the city.

Late one morning, Emperor Akbar decided to go on one of his rambles through the city. He loved to feel the pulse of the city and spend time among his subjects.

He shed his beautiful royal sherwani and chose a simple mustard kurta. He took off his kingly turban, adorned with the most beautiful jewels, and wore a simple off-white pagdi. Instead of his lavish leather jootis, he wore simple sandals. And most of all, he hid his striking moustache for a white beard that one of his servants carefully pasted on to his face.

Disguise in place, Emperor Akbar set off. Having a long train of guards with him was pointless. It would make all his efforts to disguise himself come to nought. As a rule, his many guards were forbidden from accompanying him. On foot, Emperor Akbar surreptitiously left the palace gates and mingled. He enjoyed the freedom of walking amongst his subjects.

He first had a cup of tea at a local tea shop, talking to the locals and trying to understand if they had any grievances against the crown. He then walked through the market to make sure that prices of vegetables and goods were under control. He made his way past the local school, to make sure the children were all safely in class. Then, he walked into his favourite part of the city – the town square.

This space was always bustling. There were thousands of people just going about their business. Hawkers dotted the pavements, selling their wares from colourful carts and wicker baskets. There were children playing in the little ground at the centre, while their parents lined the sides, talking to each other. There was a guru, clad in saffron, preaching to about ten people sitting at his feet. The sound of the azaan (call to prayer) floated over the houses.

But, there was one thing that had drawn the entire square's attention. A group of behrupiyas

had taken over a corner of the square. Emperor Akbar drifted into this crowd. This particular group of behrupiyas had travelled all the way from Rajasthan, and they were masters at what they did. A ringmaster was introducing each creature who stepped into the circle.

First came a learned judge, then a monkey. In no time, they both took off their disguises and out came two perfectly talented actors from beneath the makeup and clothes. There were

loud cries of disbelief from the audience. Then there was the ape that juggled and a clown who contorted his body into strange shapes. The crowd was mesmerized and Emperor Akbar was truly dumbstruck by the talent of these performers.

Just as he was thinking about how he must invite this troupe to perform in his court, the ringmaster announced the main event.

"And now ... the event we have all been waiting for! Put your hands together to welcome the highlight of today," he yelled into a megaphone. The applause was thunderous.

Out ran a bull from behind the tarpaulin, which hid the troupe from the audience. From every angle, the bull looked real. It was amazing! He stood, lifted his head towards the sky and twitched his nose disdainfully. He caught the eye of various audience members and stared them down. Every now and then, he threw his head back and snorted regally. The ringmaster grabbed a bale of hay and put it down in front of the bull. Astonishingly, the bull bent down and started eating it, chewing it thoughtfully.

The audience roared in disbelief. The crowd was in raptures. This was truly a remarkable performance. Which person would chew hay for an act? Emperor Akbar could not believe his eyes.

"This performer could walk into a meadow, mingle with a herd of bulls, and the bulls would just keep munching on their straw, and not realize that it was a human standing right in their midst!" he thought.

As he looked around at the crowd of faces gathered around the performers, he smiled. "My people are happy," he thought, with a satisfied look on his face. Then his eyes fell upon a man

looking morose. He was deep in thought, still mesmerized by the act, but frowning. "Something is troubling this gentleman," thought Emperor Akbar to himself. "I'm going to keep an eye on him."

As the crowd clapped for the bull, he waved his horns in the air and started backing up into the backstage area. The crowd quietened down in anticipation of the next act. Suddenly, the morose man Emperor Akbar had spotted bent down, picked up a small pebble and threw it at the left hind leg of the bull. The pebble hit the bull exactly where he had aimed it and fell to the ground. As it struck, the bull's skin contorted. It paused, shook its hind leg ever so slightly and then walked on.

"BRAVO! Amazing! Stupendous!" the man shouted at the performer. By now, the rest of the crowd had grown silent while the man stood out due to his loud praise. He was rapturous. "Why aren't the rest of you clapping? These behrupiyas deserve it! Come on! Come on!" he cheered and clapped.

"Tsk tsk! This boy has lost his marbles," said an old man, shaking his head, as he walked away.

"I'm not so sure," thought Emperor Akbar.

He took the gentleman aside and spoke to him.

"Tell me, young man. Why did you throw a stone at that performer while he was leaving?"

"Well, it is like this, Sir," replied the man. "It is easy to disguise oneself. Any person with even a little bit of skill can trick an audience. But when I threw that stone, the bull actually twitched his skin ever so slightly and shook his leg. Exactly like a real bull. It takes a lot of practice and skill to behave so instinctively – to stay so true to the role. Very few performers can perfect their art to be able to even mimic an animal's reflexes. It was truly amazing."

"And that is why you clapped so loudly?" asked Emperor Akbar.

"Exactly, Sir."

"You seem like an extremely intelligent man. What is your name?" asked Emperor Akbar.

"Birbal, Sir," came the response.

"Well, Birbal, will you come and work for me?" asked Emperor Akbar.

"Of course, Jahanpanah! How could a man like me refuse a royal order?" came the prompt reply.

Emperor Akbar was shocked. He had taken such care to disguise himself that morning. How could this man have known it was him?

"But ... How did you know I ... was ... am ... the emperor?"

"Well, Sire, your disguise was perfect. I am sure to the untrained eye you are some sort of commoner in their midst. I'm sure many have mistaken you for a person like any other in this crowd. But Sire, you are so regal in your body language. The nobility in the way you speak is unmistakable. I could spot you from a mile away, Jahapanah," replied Birbal, bowing low.

The next morning, a new minister entered Emperor Akbar's court. As Birbal was introduced to the courtiers, they wondered how a humble gentleman had ended up in His Majesty's court. Little did they know that, in no time, this humble gentleman would become one of the Nine Gems of Akbar – nine of his most trusted courtiers and closest confidants.

TENALI RAMAN FOILS THE THIEVES

The reign of King Krishnadevaraya was significant in many ways. Not only did he rule over one of the largest empires in Indian history, and have a number of military campaigns and successes to his name, he also ensured that literature, art and culture flourished in his kingdom. He was a poet himself, and so he truly valued the arts. He donated generously to artists, sculptors, temples and writers.

Raman of Tenali had been appointed as one of the court jesters of the Vijayanagara empire. From the time he was chosen, he had grown in his role. His wit and poetry amused, entertained and moved the lords and noble people of the court. He had become a favourite of King Krishnadevaraya.

The king had been so pleased with Raman that, often, he would reach into his cummerbund and grab a few gold coins for him. Raman, ever the frugal and wise man, saved up diligently. He soon had enough money to buy himself a house.

Not just any house but the house of his dreams. He made this his home with his beloved, aged mother and doting wife. It was something he was very proud of.

But to rise so quickly in the court of the king, Raman had to also work really hard. Most mornings, he left for the court bright and early, after eating just a few spoonfuls of rice. He often skipped lunch, and returned home well after sunset, tired, but happy. It was hard work, but he loved it.

Even on days when there was no court, or when the king was away at a royal retreat, Raman had no break. He had become well known for his gift of thought and people from across the empire would come to consult with him.

On his days of rest, Raman was busy with tasks in his own home. He spent the day fixing things in his home, such as a minor leak, putting up a new picture frame, painting a chipped wall.

However, his true love was his garden. In the short time that Raman had owned the house, he had grown little lemon trees, and shrubs of curry leaves and coriander. He had sown rice in one corner and had lovingly tended to beautiful banyan trees and a grand peepal tree at the very centre of his garden. His garden was his pride and joy, and he spent every moment that he could spare in it.

One evening, Raman was returning home from the king's court, well into the night. As the moon shone upon the path that led to his

home, his head was awash with thoughts of his garden.

He remembered that he had not watered his plants all week. He worried that the weaker saplings he had planted were going to die, while some of his other plants might have already frayed. It upset him.

As he approached his home, Raman decided that he would wake up earlier than usual the next morning and water his garden.

Just then, he noticed two shadowy figures lurking behind some trees. in a corner of his garden.

He knew exactly what they were up to. That morning the discussion at court had only been around the band of thieves in the city. The king had been furious.

"This has got to stop!" he had bellowed.

He had promptly drawn up an action plan to police the streets to try to put an end to the criminal activity. But royal

decrees don't travel down to ground level as quickly as you would expect.

Raman took one look at those two shadowy figures lurking in his garden and knew that his home would be broken into next. He had to think fast.

As soon as Raman entered his home, he yelled at his wife and said, "Dinner can wait. The city is ridden with thieves! King Krishnadevaraya has advised everyone to hide or lock up all their valuables immediately. TONIGHT! Let's attend to that first."

In all the years they had been married, Raman had never shouted at his wife. She knew something was wrong immediately.

"Oh dear!" said Raman's wife. "I had no idea. This is such bad news. I'm worried about our safety. I am so careless, I don't even latch the door till we are about to go to sleep. What should we do?"

"Look, where is the trunk? Let me go fetch it. In the meantime, gather all the silver and gold, the money and your jewellery. We will put it ..." said Raman.

"Yes? Where can we put it? Maybe we can put it under the bed?" his wife suggested.

"No! No! That would be too obvious. It would be the first place a thief would look."

"Then where?" asked his wife.

"Got it! When I bring the trunk down, you place all the valuables in it and I will carry it to the well."

"The well?" asked his wife, clearly surprised

"Yes, think about it! The thieves would look everywhere inside our home, in every nook and corner. But will they ever think to check at the bottom of a well?"

"You are so clever!" replied his wife, with admiration in her eyes.

"Ha! Ha! That's what you think!" thought one of the thieves, who, just as Raman had thought, stood quietly by the window, listening to every word.

Raman had spoken loudly to make sure the eavesdroppers caught every word. The two thieves looked at each other with glee.

"He's saved us so much time. We don't even need to look for the gold!" thought one of the thieves,

with a huge smile on his face.

Raman stepped closer to his wife and whispered, "There are two thieves outside. I am trying to dupe them. Find something really heavy. I'll go get the trunk."

Soon, Raman brought the trunk out from the bedroom. He loudly huffed and puffed as he placed it on the kitchen floor. His wife, who had developed a keen understanding of her husband's ways over the years, had promptly gone into the kitchen and looked around. Her eye fell on the grinding stone.

"Perfect! This will be ideal!" she whispered to herself, as she carefully rolled it out and placed it inside the trunk.

Under cover of darkness, but with loud grunts and groans to alert the thieves of what was happening, Raman dragged the trunk to the well. There, he raised it and carefully leaned it against the walls of the well. He took in a deep breath and then with a giant shout and a huge heave, he pushed the trunk into the well.

SPLASH!

"And now for a good night's sleep!" Raman said aloud to himself, fully aware that the thieves would hear him.

The two thieves had, of course, greedily watched everything unfold. They patiently waited as Raman went back inside and the family ate. They could hear the dishes being cleared and washed. With barely concealed glee, they watched as all the lamps in the house were blown out one by one. Then, they waited till they could hear the occasional, faint rumble of snoring from inside the house and nothing more.

The time was ripe for robbery! They both gleefully walked to the well and quietly peered into it.

"It doesn't seem like there's too much water in there," said the first thief.

"That just makes our job easier! Let's drain all the water out of the well. Then all we have to do is lift the trunk from the bed," responded the other, with an evil grin on his face.

The two thieves got to work. They pulled up bucket after bucket of water, all night long.

And guess what they did with the water?

They emptied each bucket of water into the garden; the same one that Raman was so proud of.

They were so busy working that they did not notice the sky rapidly change colour.

"The sun will rise soon! The sound of the birds chirping will wake up the people in the home!" said one thief, with urgency.

"Let's hurry up!" said the other.

The thieves started rushing.

Splish! Splash! Splosh!

Water splashed all around them, making everything slippery and making their task so much harder.

"UGH! My back hurts! Can you see the trunk yet?" asked one of the thieves.

"No. Not as yet! Come on! Don't give up! I'm sure we're nearly there! There can't be much more. We're nearly there ... we're nearly there ..." came the reply.

Soon, Raman was awake and he excitedly shook his wife awake. As they both stood at the window, they could still see two figures, in the distance, tirelessly working at the well.

"And, my garden is watered!" said Raman, contentedly.

His wife laughed with delight.

GOPAL IN THE SWEET SHOP

Gopal Bhar was the jester in the court of Raja Krishnachandra, the King of Nadia. The capital of the kingdom was Krishnanagar, and this was where Gopal lived.

Gopal was beloved in Krishnanagar. The king loved his antics, the courtiers were all amused at his showmanship and the people of the city adored his ways. But his real fans, the ones who truly appreciated him, were the children.

You see, Gopal was always in close touch with the child inside him and he never thought it beneath himself to spend time with the kids in his city. They adored him and he adored them.

Every so often, Gopal would find himself playing with the children of Krishnanagar. He was an excellent hide-and-seek player, and wasn't too bad at hopscotch, when his old knees allowed him to play. But what he really enjoyed, more than the games, were the pranks. He would regularly set booby traps for the hapless townspeople with his cohort of little friends. Or they would play practical jokes, scaring their

friends and making elaborate hoaxes to cause panic all over the city.

One afternoon, Gopal found himself in the company of these children. The kids had been playing all morning and were hungry.

"Gopal Uncle!" the oldest one said. "Will you do something for us? Please?"

"I'm sure he will!" said another.

"Go on ... let me hear it!" said Gopal, smiling.

"Will you get us some free sweets from Bhola's shop?" said the boy.

"Oh! That isn't even possible! Bhola never gives anything for free," replied one of the boys.

"Yeah, he will let his sweets rot, before he gives them to us!" said another.

"But what can we do? His sweets are the best in the city!" piped up a third.

"He cheats us, even when we're willing to pay full price for the sweets!" said the fourth, with disgust.

"Is that so?" asked Gopal. "Hmmm ..."

Gopal loved many things in life. He loved a good laugh. He loved to make others laugh. He enjoyed the company of intelligent people who would test his wits. He truly enjoyed a good fish and rice meal. But his one true love, the pinnacle of all that was good in his life, was a good sweet.

The idea of a finely balanced mishti doi (sweetened yoghurt) or a juicy rasgulla would make his head spin. But of all the sweets in the world, it was Krishnanagar's own sarpuriya that was his favourite. This was beautiful sweet that combined kheer, cottage cheese and thick cream. Gopal's mouth watered just thinking about it. And guess where they could get the very best sarpuriya in all of Krishnanagar?

That's right. In Bhola's sweet shop.

Therefore, the heist that the kids were pushing Gopal to pull off became extra sweet in his mind. He felt his tummy rumble just a little.

With a smile on his face, Gopal announced, "You leave Bhola to me, kids. And get ready for a mighty feast! I'll be back soon."

With a bounce in his step, Gopal marched up to Bhola's shop. Gopal knew that it was customary for Bhola to have a little siesta after his lunch. Gopal also knew that this was the best time to strike. He patiently waited outside, peeking in frequently to check if Bhola was going to take his afternoon break.

"I'm going for my nap now, boy. You watch over every sweet in the shop," Bhola bellowed at his son, who had just been hired as his assistant. "Watch out for those pesky kids and don't you dare go dipping your hands in for a sneaky one, you hear me? I have counted every last one. So,

I'll know if any are missing."

"O-okay, father," the frightened boy meekly stammered. "I'll do that."

As soon as Bhola was asleep, in marched Gopal. He stared at all the sweets around him, inspecting each one. Then, as the boy kept a watchful eye on him, he slowly dipped his hand into the tray of sarpuriya. He picked one up and, in a giant gulp, wolfed it down. Then he grabbed another. And then another! Fast as lightning, his hand went back and forth.

"STOP!" yelled the young boy, in utter panic. The boy had just joined his father's business and had never met Gopal. "What are you doing? Who are you? Stop!"

"Oh! You don't recognize me?" asked Gopal, who was now shovelling mishti doi into his mouth with his left hand, while grabbing a tray of sandesh with his right. "Don't worry, my child. Your father knows me very well."

"Umm ... I don't, Sir," cried the boy. "Who are you?"

"My name is Maachhi. Maachhi Da to you! How very nice to meet you," said Gopal with a twinkle in his eye. 'Maacchi' meant fly in Bengali, and Gopal was trying hard to control his laughter.

But even as he was saying this, he was busy. He had emptied all the mishti doi from a giant pot and was now filling it to the brim with other gorgeous treats. All the while, for every sweet he put in the pot, he put two in his own mouth.

"Father! Father! Wake up!" the boy ran out of the shop towards his father's room. "Come quickly. Maachhi Da has come."

Bhola had been rudely awakened and was annoyed. "What are you saying, boy? Why don't you let me rest? Stop chattering and allow me to go back to sleep!"

"But, father, Maachhi Da is eating the sweets!"

"What do you mean eating the sweets? How much can a maachhi eat? Stop being silly and

use your head, boy! Now go away and don't disturb me," said Bhola rudely, turning around and going right back to sleep.

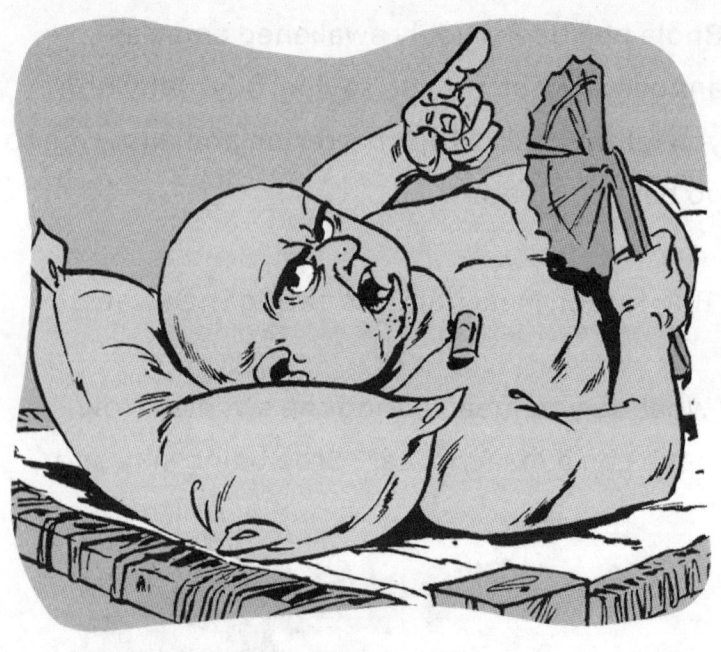

And so the boy came back to the shop reluctantly and said, "Father seems to think it is okay. So, I suppose it is okay, Maachhi Da. Enjoy the sweets!"

"See? I told you, your father wouldn't mind if I came here and helped myself to this," said Gopal, as he grabbed one more piece of sandesh on his way out. "Oh, and let's not forget this one!"

Soon, Gopal was surrounded by the children. "Well, kids, here you are!" said Gopal, passing around the giant pot of sweets.

"Gopal Uncle! You are amazing!" said one child.

"My God! You got so many sweets from Bhola?" asked another.

"How?" questioned a third.

"Yes! Tell us how you did it!" demanded a fourth.

Gopal stood smugly, lapping up the attention.

"Hahahaha! A magician never reveals his tricks, boys! Now enjoy the sweets. And remember to thank Bhola every time you go to his shop. Oh, and also, give him Maachhi Da's regards."

THE CORRUPT OFFICIAL

It was a busy day at Emperor Akbar's court. As he sat on the throne, the courtiers lounged around him, contemplating the day's work.

Birbal was deep in thought. He had been grappling with a problem to do with the state's treasury and had avoided getting involved in the matters of the day. It was a quiet day, like any other. Nothing much seemed to be happening. However, this would soon change.

"Jahanpanah!" said a voice. "Pardon the intrusion."

A senior policeman of Agra, escorting a prisoner, stood before the emperor.

"Go ahead," responded Emperor Akbar.

"Sire, I have brought this man from the granary. He was the official in-charge there. We had a tip off that he was accepting bribes from corrupt merchants. So, I sent a constable in plain clothes to pretend to be a merchant buying grain to sell in Delhi. He was caught red-handed, Jahanpanah! We have arrested him."

"Hmmm ..." said Emperor Akbar, as he stroked his chin. "Right. Take him away and keep him in the holding cells. We will try him later."

A short while later, Emperor Akbar turned to Birbal.

"Birbal, I have often wondered how corruption works. Do you think there are certain jobs that make a person corrupt or is it that some people are inherently corrupt and will do bad things regardless of the position they hold? What I mean is, is it the job that corrupts the person or vice versa?"

"Jahanpanah, I think it is the person that corrupts a job," replied Birbal. "If a person is corrupt, it does not matter what they do. He will find a way to illegally benefit from it – whether it be taking bribes, taking short cuts or just generally shirking work."

"I beg to differ, Jahanpanah!" piped up a voice. It was Abdullah, one of Birbal's rivals who had spoken up.

Birbal had always regarded Abdullah as a petty and dull man. He had inherited his place in Akbar's court from his father but had never really made a significant contribution. He was jealous of Birbal, for being a self-made man, for making his way into the highest court in the land and for quickly becoming one of Akbar's most prized courtiers.

"I believe that it is the job that makes a person corrupt," Abdullah continued. "I can think of a hundred jobs in which there isn't a chance for a person to take bribes."

"Can you name just one?" challenged Birbal, raising his eyebrows.

"Hmmm ... let me think ..."

"Go on ..." said Emperor Akbar, intrigued.

"Jahanpanah," said the man proudly, as a brilliant idea struck him. "Ask the man you've just arrested to sit on the banks of the river Jamuna and count the number of ripples on the water. I am sure that this is a job where bribery is out of the question." He had a victorious smile on his face as he glanced at Birbal.

"If you can even call that a job!" replied Birbal, with a laugh. "But I will be happy if this can reform a corrupt man, Jahanpanah. I, however, do not think that even this scheme will work."

"Fine, let us test it out," said Emperor Akbar as he turned to his first minister. "Make sure that the man we arrested from the granary is put to this new 'work' immediately."

And so, the man was stationed on a rock on the banks of the Jamuna, and instructed on his new job. He was puzzled, but since it beat sitting in jail, he asked no questions.

A week passed. As Emperor Akbar sat on his throne in court that morning, the first thing he said was, "Whatever happened to the man who was counting ripples for us? The corrupt man from the granary? I wonder how he is doing. Do you have any updates, minister?"

The first minister stood up.

"Jahanpanah, the report is that the man is still on the job. He has been sitting on the banks of the river, religiously counting the ripples on the water."

The emperor turned to Birbal. "It seems Abdullah was right, Birbal. There are indeed some jobs that cannot corrupt an individual."

"Sire, I still disagree," said Birbal. "May I suggest checking on him ourselves?"

"Oh Birbal! Just admit you are wrong," said Abdullah, trying hard to be gracious but unable to wipe the smirk off his face.

"No, Abdullah," interjected Emperor Akbar. "It's not a bad idea. Let us go and see for ourselves. If he is indeed incorrect, I am sure Birbal is not above recognizing his mistake. Isn't that so, Birbal? Wouldn't you agree?"

"Jahanpanah, I will gladly accept my mistake in this matter if I am proved wrong," replied Birbal, with a slight bow of his head.

"Then let us all go right now," said Abdullah. "Or should we plan this for tomorrow?"

"No, now," replied Birbal. " But let us disguise ourselves. Let us test him as if we're members of the public! The three of us can pretend to be poor fishermen approaching the bank."

"Birbal, you know how much I love disguises! Let's do this!" said Emperor Akbar.

Soon, Emperor Akbar, Birbal and Abdullah were on the royal pier, on the banks of the river Jamuna, waiting to board a boat. Not in a hundred years, would anyone have been able to recognize them.

The emperor had on his favourite fake beard and was dressed in a ragged green kurta, whereas Birbal was in a torn blue kurta and a yellow pagdi. A faint beard adorned his cheeks. Abdulla, not having shaved, wore a light pink kurta, grey dhoti and white pagdi.

Birbal had chosen an old fishing boat to take them, instead of Akbar's usual grand yacht. They all carried nets and looked exactly like local fishermen on their boat.

The three set off. Birbal and Abdullah rowed and the emperor guided them.

As they approached the bank in question, Akbar spotted the corrupt official. He was seated on a rock and looked hard at work.

"There he is! A little to the left now!" commanded Emperor Akbar, in a low voice.

The three of them were almost at the shore. The corrupt official, who had been bent over his notebook marking each ripple, got distracted.

"How dare you come here! Can't you see I am on official duty? Now you have distracted me," he fumed.

"We are so sorry, Huzoor," shouted Birbal from the boat. "We're just trying to come ashore here."

"Well, you've made me lose my count. Don't you know who I am?"

"Who are you, Sir?" shouted Emperor Akbar. "Why can't we be here?"

"I am on duty for the Jahanpanah! I am to sit here and count the ripples on the water. You three have made me lose count now. This is a crime! I will complain to the first minister and you three we will be jailed for a whole year," replied the corrupt official.

"Jail, Huzoor?" asked Abdullah, pretending to look scared and widening his eyes.

"Yes! Jail! I will report you. Unless …" Even in his anger, the corrupt official saw an opportunity. His tone changed. "Well, unless you can give me a hundred gold coins."

"A hundred gold coins, Sir? We are poor fishermen. We don't have that kind of money. Here, take this bag of coins. It is all we have. It has fifty gold coins," replied Birbal.

"Fifty? No! I must have a hundred," replied the greedy man.

"A hundred he shall have then!" said Akbar, as he removed his fake beard. "One hundred lashes!"

"Jahanpanah! It's you!" the man exclaimed, shocked. "Sire? Sire? Please forgive me. I ... I ..."

"Stop grovelling! Birbal, you are right. This is a corrupt man. Abdullah, there is no job that this man will do honestly. He will have to be jailed," said Emperor Akbar, in an icy tone.

"Yes, Sire. Birbal was indeed right," responded Abdullah, meekly. "Why does he always have to be right?" he grumbled under his breath.

"Pardon me?" said the emperor.

"Nothing, Sire! Nothing! I was just saying, Birbal is always right," said Abdullah hurriedly and with fake enthusiasm. "Always right."

TENALI AND THE HORSE'S MOUTH

Raman of Tenali's wit and wisdom had become renowned. Stories of King Krishnadevaraya's favourite jester had spread far and wide, within his empire, and beyond.

Raman had not been traditionally trained or taught. By virtue of his station in life, he had never received any formal education. Instead, he had received his wisdom from the world around him. He was observant and had soaked in knowledge from everything he saw and everyone he met. He had learnt from his experiences, not from the scriptures that the other scholars in the king's court held so dear.

Despite this, or maybe because of it, Raman shone bright in court. He won debates with his intelligence and quick wit. He gave the king the wisest counsel in the form of a joke. It was clear that Raman was no plain jester. He had fast become an extremely important member of King Krishnadevaraya's inner circle.

Raman's proximity to the king and his ever-growing popularity did not, however, go unnoticed. It gave rise to a lot of jealousy within the court. Whispers surrounded Raman.

"How can this fool, who seemed to have strayed into the court just yesterday, become so close to the king?"

"Why should we even listen to this jester?"

"Why is King Krishnadevaraya listening to him over our scholars?"

"He's not even properly educated. What hold does he have over the king?"

In the middle of these whispers was Panditraj. Panditraj had taken Raman's wit as a personal attack. He was the greatest scholar in King Krishnadevaraya's court; the most learned man in the land.

"Can this silly jester be wiser than me?" he

privately asked his confidantes, stroking his long, grey beard thoughtfully.

Almost every day at court, some minister or scholar or poet would try to pit their wit against Raman's. And every single time, they would be defeated in the kindest, softest way by Raman of Tenali.

One day, the court was in full swing, when a trader from Arabia arrived. Traders and merchants would arrive in the Vijayanagara court with the finest merchandise in the world, knowing full well that King Krishnadevaraya's generosity and desire for quality were second to none.

"Your Majesty, I have come from the distant shores of Arabia with one hundred of the finest horses in our lands. These are from our best stables, Sire. These are the most valuable horses in the world. Horses from Arabia are world-renowned," said the trader.

"Very well," said King Krishnadevaraya. "I shall buy the entire lot. Bring them to the palace courtyard this afternoon."

"You are too kind, Your Majesty. Thank you," said the trader, bowing his head. "It shall be done."

That afternoon, all the courtiers gathered in the courtyard outside.

"Indeed, these are fine horses," King Krishnadevaraya said, admiring his purchase. "They are strong and swift-footed."

He then turned to his courtiers, and said, "Each one of you shall take a horse home with you. For a month, you shall look after the horse as though it is your own. You shall train your horse to make it the fastest horse in the land. I am sure these fine beasts will be up to the task. At the end of the month, there will be a grand race. The master of the winning horse will receive a handsome reward!"

"You are too kind, Maharaj!"

"Jai King Krishnadevaraya!"

"All hail the King!"

Cries rang out in the air.

King Krishnadevaraya and Panditraj allotted a horse to each courtier. After the courtiers had

all led their horses away, and the king was about to retire, Raman spoke up.

"Ahem, Maharaj? I beg your pardon. But why have I not been allotted a horse?"

Panditraj, ever ready to put Raman in his place, barked back, "What would a fool know about training horses? That's why!"

"But, Sire ..."

"Panditraj is right, Raman. I don't think you have it in you to train a horse," said the king.

Raman was not about to accept defeat. "Please, Maharaj, give me a chance. If I try, Sire, I am confident I will succeed."

"Hmmm ... Very well ... All right. Panditraj, let Raman be given a horse as well," announced the king, with finality in his voice. Panditraj did not argue.

As Panditraj handed the reigns of the horse to Raman, Raman smiled widely. "You will see, Sir. I will train this horse better than you think."

With that, Raman of Tenali, now the proud guardian of one of the finest horses in the world, led it home.

When Raman got home, he tied his horse in his garden, and started to build him a stable. On the first day, he built the first wall, on the second, the second wall and on the third the third wall. But instead of stopping here as one would

For a normal stable, Raman of Tenali built a fourth wall. It now looked like the strangest stable any person would ever lay their eyes on!

The horse was trapped on all four sides, by walls! There was only one small opening, just large enough for the horse to put its head through and receive its daily ration of hay.

Day after day, the horse remained in this stable, trapped on all sides except for that little window. Raman did not wash it, train it or even talk to it. Every day, Raman would come to the window and feed the horse. That was it.

A month later, the whole city arrived to witness the race. A special pavilion was built for the

king and all the courtiers gathered. The Arabian horses looked grand. They were dressed in fine silks and leather saddles. They had all been fed, had shiny coats and looked like true race horses, raring to go!

The king arrived. "Panditraj, are all the horses gathered?" he asked.

"All but Raman's, Maharaj. I knew he ..." but the king had raised his hand. Panditraj stopped.

"Raman!" shouted the king, angrily. "Where is your horse?"

"Maharaj!" replied a snivelling Raman. "That

horse is such a ferocious beast! He scares me! I dare not go near it!"

"I do not believe him, Maharaj!" shouted Panditraj, sensing an opportunity. "He hasn't trained his horse well enough and now he's ashamed of it. This is why Raman is hiding the poor thing! This is all just an excuse."

"Is that so?" questioned King Krishnadevaraya.

"Maharaj, I don't lie," pleaded Raman. "I really dare not go near it!"

"That is a horrible excuse, Maharaj!" cried Panditraj. "For all we know, Raman might have even sold it!"

"That is an awful accusation! Raman, what do you have to say for yourself?" asked the king.

"Maharaj," came the reply. "I am hurt. I have not sold the horse. If Panditraj does not believe me, he can come to my home and see for himself."

"Very well," said the king. "Go, Panditraj, and see the horse for yourself. Bring it here to me. I want to see this fierce beast with my own eyes!"

"If it is the last thing I do, Maharaj, I will do as you say. I will personally lead this horse to you, that is, if it's even there!" vowed Panditraj.

So, through the winding streets of the city, Panditraj grumbled.

"You are up to one of your tricks again, Raman. I can feel it. I do not trust you. What have you done? Tell me the truth. I bet you've sold the horse and now you're going to show me some painting of a horse or a horse made out of clay or something even more fanciful. Am I correct?"

"Panditraj, I respect you so very much! Why won't you believe me?" said Raman, as they approached his home.

"Fine! Where is this horse of yours? Show me!" demanded Panditraj.

"Right there! In the stable," said Raman, pointing at the absurd shelter he had built for the horse.

"Raman! You fool! Do you call that a stable?" said an infuriated Panditraj.

"Panditraj, please don't be angry. You know that I am an uneducated man. I am not as learned as you are. This is what I thought a stable should look like. I didn't know any better."

Inside the stable, the horse had heard Raman's voice. For an entire month, the horse had had no contact with any man or beast, apart from Raman, and that too, only when Raman had fed it hay. It neighed and hoofed, and excitedly paced about in his stable. The horse was making a rather loud racket.

"There! See? It even sounds ferocious, does it not?" asked Raman, as he pointed at the stable.

"Just stop talking and let me see the horse!" demanded Panditraj.

"This way! Here, look through this window. You can see it from here. But be warned, Panditraj, this is a dangerous horse!"

"Oh, step out of the way, fool!" shouted Panditraj as he peered in through the window.

Now, the horse had not seen another creature in a month, remember? It looked at the face that presented itself through the window, and saw the long, grey beard on Panditraj's face. Not knowing what it was, the horse decided that the beard was the closest thing to hay that it could find.

So, the horse did what all horses do when they see hay. It took a massive bite. But once its teeth were locked into the beard, it realized that this was not what it was used to. So it got upset and refused to let go!

OWWWWWWWWWWWWW!

A howl shattered the peace of the day. "Raman!" screamed Panditraj. "RAMAN! HELP ME!"

"I dare not, Panditraj!" came the quiet response. "I did warn you, didn't I? That beast is ferocious and strong as a ... well ... horse, I suppose. That's what I was telling you all this while, Panditraj. I wish you had believed me."

Soon, a crowd had gathered. The local pehlwan was the first to try. He yanked at poor Panditraj, stuck to the window of the stable, but to no avail.

"OWWWWWWWWWWW!" Panditraj continued to wail.

Then three men tried pulling Panditraj free. But this was one of the strongest horses in the herd that had arrived from Arabia. It was not about to let go.

"I suppose there is no alternative," said one of the courtiers who had made his way there. "We must break down the walls of this stable."

"Then let's break them down!" yelled the city-folk as they scrambled to find their tools.

Soon, four men were hacking at the walls while poor Panditraj stayed there with dust flying all around him.

Finally, the stable was broken down and the learned scholar was free ... well, almost.

Because while the walls fell in shambles around his feet, guess where his beard was? Still in the horse's mouth!

"Oh Lord! What am I to do now? This wretched beast just won't let go! What do I do?" screamed a panicked Panditraj.

"Well, Panditraj," said the courtier. "This IS the king's horse. Only the king can take a decision on what is to be done."

"True," said Raman. "And you did promise to lead the horse to Maharaj, remember?"

"Lead it, yes!" replied poor Panditraj. "BUT NOT BY MY BEARD!"

"Sorry, Panditraj," said the courtier. "But I see no other alternative. Let us go!"

The city was treated to the strangest sight it had ever seen.

A man, walking backwards, leading a horse, who was biting his beard!

"What on earth is going on?"

"Isn't that Panditraj?"

"What is he doing?"

"Is Panditraj leading the horse or is the horse leading Panditraj?"

"What a cruel fellow? What is he trying to do to that poor horse?"

The citizens came out of their homes and shops and lined the street as this strange procession went through.

At last, the procession reached the palace grounds. Raman walked up to the king, with poor Panditraj wailing in the background.

"Maharaj, I present my horse …"

Wild laughter broke out. King Krishnadevaraya had never seen a more absurd sight. He too doubled over with laughter.

"Maharaj! Please, Sire!" pleaded Panditraj. "I do not know what to do! Please free me from the jaws of this cruel, vicious creature!"

"All right. Enough! Raman, enough of your pranks! Free him!" ordered a still smiling King Krishnadevaraya.

"I beg your pardon, Maharaj. I'll do that," said Raman as he turned towards Panditraj. "Get me a pair of scissors!"

"NOOOOOO!" cried an aghast Panditraj. "Please don't cut my beard, Raman."

"Fine. But do you believe me now, Panditraj?"

"I do! I do! I will never doubt you again, Raman! Just get me out of here."

"Fine! You there," ordered Raman to one of the guards. "Get me some hay!"

As soon as the hay arrived, Raman picked up some and waved it in front of the horse's nose. Immediately, it let go of the beard and grabbed the hay.

Panditraj had his freedom back and stood in the corner, both defeated and relieved. The horse stood peacefully, eating his hay, and Raman stood in the corner, smiling.

"So, Raman has won again, I see," thought the king. But King Krishnadevaraya was as skilled at politics as he was in statecraft. He knew that he could not be seen to be partial towards Raman.

"Raman, this time you have gone too far. I cannot tolerate this kind of insult to my beloved

Panditraj. Please go and never show me your face again!" said the king, gravely.

As he watched his beloved jester leave, the king thought, "I wish he hadn't gone so far with this joke. I have to send him away. He crossed a line. But I will miss him."

The king slept fitfully that night, upset at what had happened. The next morning, the king was still groggy when he opened his eyes. Just as he could focus, he was greeted by an unusual sight.

There was a person standing in the corner of the room, with a pot on his head and two perfectly cut out eyes! Fear gripped him.

"Who is this? Who are you? GUARDS!" cried the king.

"Don't be scared, Your Majesty. It is I, Raman!"

Now the king's fear gave way to anger.

"Raman? What are you doing here? I told you never to show me your face again!"

Pat came the response, "But that is why I have covered it, Maharaj!"

The king burst out laughing. He walked over to Raman and removed the pot himself.

"Even the gods themselves cannot match your wit, Raman! May you live long!"

Raman bent his head and received his king's blessings, happy in the knowledge that he would continue to serve.

GOPAL AND THE PETTY THIEF

Krishnanagar, where Gopal lived, was a dacoit-infested area. They were well-organized, with very well-rehearsed plans to rob entire areas of the city. They had elevated this terrible crime to an artform.

The entire city feared and dreaded them. The king had put in place stringent measures, with the police force and the royal guards taking nightly rounds. But the dacoits seemed to know where they were scheduled to check each night and dodged them.

In all this large scale mischief, the lowly petty thief had been ignored. The one who acted alone and took a thing or two from a house that he had targeted. The police force had been so completely focussed on rooting out the system of dacoity from the city that they had ignored the petty criminal.

This sounds like life was good for the petty thieves in the city but, on the contrary, they had had to starve. Each night, they would set out under cover of darkness to ply their unholy trade and, at dawn, they would have to outrun the darkness while being chased by hundreds of dacoits.

You see, the dacoits not only stole and thieved, but also carved up entire territories.

Only one group of dacoits was allowed to hit a particular area. And a petty thief who dared infiltrate it? Well, he would meet a fate far worse than their victims.

One quiet, dark night, Gopal and his wife awoke to a sudden creeping noise in their bedroom. They quickly lit a candle, and realized that a petty thief was standing right in the middle of the room.

"Hands up!" shouted the petty thief, holding a knife. "Now, hand over the keys! And be quick. I don't have all night!"

"The keys to what, Sir?" asked Gopal innocently.

"Oh! You're a funny one, aren't you? The keys to your safe."

Then, turning towards Gopal's wife, he continued, "Or better yet, just hand me all your gold, lady! I don't have time to waste."

Gopal's wife was a smart and cunning lady. But at this hour of the night, on seeing a thief with a knife in his hands standing in her bedroom, she was genuinely scared.

"Just t-t-take whatever you w-w-want!" she said, pleading. "J-j-just spare our lives! PLEASE!"

Right then, they heard a thud from outside.

"What is that?" said the petty thief, immediately alert.

"Um ... it must be another thief trying to break in," said Gopal. "You should check."

"Okay, okay!" said the petty thief, as he craned his neck to look out of the window.

"Who is it?" asked Gopal. "Can you see?"

"Hush! Stay quiet!" replied the petty thief. But his anxiety was clear.

"What is the matter?" asked Gopal, as a deep frown spread over the thief's face. "You look so worried suddenly."

"I-I-I am done for!" quivered the thief. "It is a gang of dacoits! I don't know what to do! I'm not supposed to be here. This is their territory!"
The thief suddenly fell at Gopal's feet.

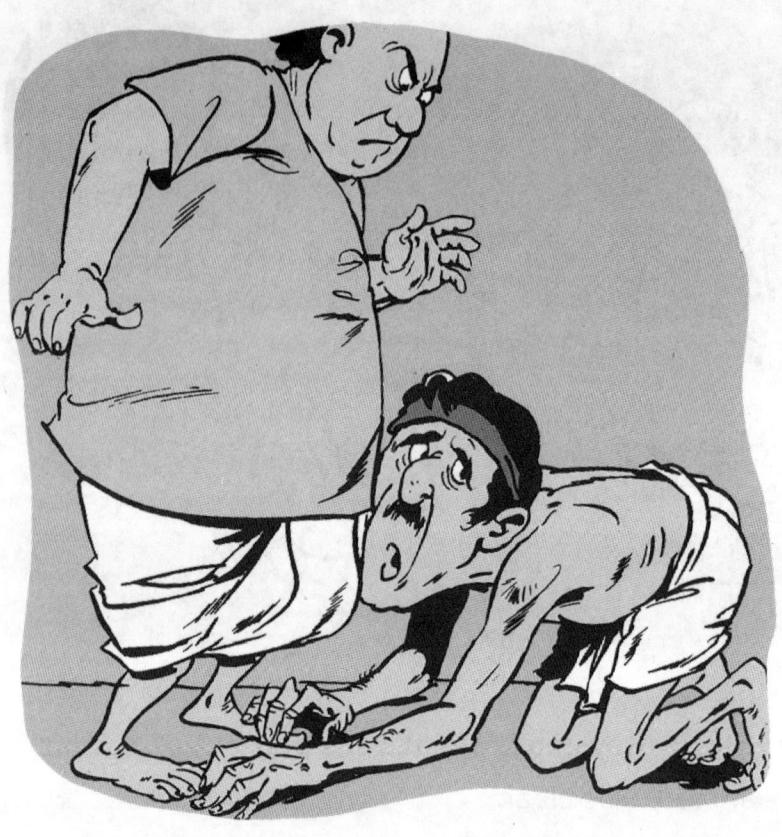

"Sir! Sir! Please, please help me. I am done for! They'll be here any moment and if they find me here, they will murder me! Please, Sir! You will have to protect me. Without your help, I am a dead man."

The thief quietly whimpered in fright, as he knelt at Gopal's feet.

"B-b-but what about us?" cried Gopal's wife in fright. "First, this thief tries to rob us and now a gang of dacoits is coming to our home? Will we even have the clothes on our back by the time dawn breaks?"

"Calm down, dear. God is protecting us. We will be fine," replied Gopal.

Then he turned to the thief.

"All right. Here's what we will do. We'll protect you. Let us find somewhere for you to hide. But you must stop panicking! What's your name?"

"Thank you! Thank you! Truly, from the bottom of my heart. Thank you, good Sir! My name is Rajesh," replied the petty thief.

"Yes, yes!" said Gopal as he dropped his voice to a whisper. "Now, both of you, please lower your voices. You don't want the dacoits to know what we're planning."

He pointed underneath the bed.

"Rajesh, you bend down and lie down under the bed. That is where you are going to hide. And remember, do not peep out! Lie still."

The thief crawled below the bed and found a corner to hide in.

"Now quickly," Gopal urgently whispered to his wife. "Come with me."

He guided his wife to a corner of the room, far from the bed, so that the thief would not hear what he was about to say.

"Listen, I am off to get the police," Gopal whispered into his wife's ear. "They will all be at the station, so it will take me a little time to go there and get them back here. Now listen carefully to what I am saying and do EXACTLY as I tell you." He whispered his plan in her ear.

Soon, Gopal left through the front door.

"Best of luck!" he said, as he walked out. "Stay strong."

"I am so scared!" responded his wife.

"Don't worry," he reassured her. "Everything will be all right."

As if on cue, just as Gopal uttered these words ...

SLAM!

The dacoits had broken through the back door!

The head robber was massive man. He wore a red bandana and sported a huge, scary moustache. Just one look at him and Gopal's wife was quivering with fear. But Gopal had a plan and she trusted her husband. She was scared, but she was intelligent and knew she could do this.

"Come on, woman! Out with all the gold and silver! Out with every precious thing you have in the house!" screamed the head robber. "DO IT NOW! If you value your life."

"B-b-but, Sir," she said meekly. "It is all locked up."

"So give me the keys!"

"B-but, Sir, they are with the master!"

"Where is the master, then?"

And then, just as planned, Gopal's wife pointed towards the bed and said, "There!"

The head dacoit bent down and looked under the bed. He saw two eyes blinking at him.

"I knew there was someone under there!" he said to his second-in-command. "Out you come! NOW!"

Without waiting, he grabbed the poor petty thief's arm and yanked! Out came the trembling, terrified man!

"Sending your wife out, while you're hiding under the bed?" said the head dacoit. "You are making my blood boil. Coward! Now where are the keys to the safe?"

"I-I-I don't have them, Sir. Believe me!"

"Believe you? Believe the snivelling coward?" He turned towards his gang. "Have you heard of anything more absurd? He wants us to believe that he is the man of the house, but doesn't have the key!"

He turned back to face the thief.

"Hand them over ... or else!" He raised his machete.

"Please! Please don't hurt me! I am not the master of this house, Sir. Believe me!" came the response from the shivering Rajesh.

THWACK!

"I do not believe you, you coward!" bellowed the infuriated dacoit. "Your wife just said …"

"My wife?" interrupted the crying thief. "Sir! I've never laid eyes on this woman before! I promise you."

"What?" shouted the head dacoit. "You are denying your own wife? I have met many scoundrels and low lives in my time, but I've never ever met anyone as awful as you before! Boys? Let's teach this fool a lesson."

The whole gang proceeded to jump on the thief and gave him a – in their opinion – well-deserved hiding.

Just then, Gopal returned. He brought with him the choicest police force.

In fact, it looked like the entire police department had marched through the city with him that night, and were right outside his home now.

"It worked!" thought Gopal as he peered through the window. "My plan worked! Oooof! But look how they're beating that poor Rajesh. I suppose I should rescue him."

Inside the room, Rajesh cowered, protecting his poor head, as he expected the next blow. But suddenly, it all stopped.

The door burst open. The dacoits were taken by surprise as the policemen rushed into the room. Gopal's plan had worked!

The dacoits were lined up, arrested and led to jail. Just as they were leaving, the head policeman looked over and counted ...

"Gopal Sir?" he said. "You had told us about some petty thief who had also come to your house. Where is he?"

"Oh! The master, you mean?" quipped Gopal's wife. "Let's leave him alone, dear. He's been punished enough for his crimes!"

THE WISE ANSWER

It was the end of a very long day at court. The day had been spent discussing matters of granaries and iron smelting, horses and armouries. There were new roads to be built and a bridge to be repaired. There was the monastery on the eastern reaches of the kingdom that needed an urgent grant and there was the Turkish king's emissary to entertain. The court had taken only a short break for lunch and everyone was tired. It was now almost time for dinner.

Emperor Akbar and his courtiers all looked exhausted. The emperor found his mind wandering to thoughts of the raga he would request over dinner. He thought of the mutton laden with ghee, the dal full of dry fruits and the mango that he would have for dessert. His stomach rumbled loudly. He casually glanced at the clock.

"Enough!" Emperor Akbar finally announced. "It has been a long day and I am sure you are all as tired as I am. We can break for the day and take up all the other matters tomorrow."

"Jahanpanah," interjected the court usher humbly. "I am sorry for the intrusion, but there is a pundit who has arrived and requested an audience with you. He has travelled all the way from Madurai, in the hope of witnessing your wisdom and Birbal's wit. He is scheduled to leave for Madurai tomorrow. What do you wish for me to tell him, Sire?"

"Hmmm ..." thought Emperor Akbar. "I am very tired. Can't this wait for tomorrow? Then again, it isn't good form to shun a pundit. I don't want the king of Madurai to be upset."

"Let him in," the emperor ordered the usher. "Birbal, please stay. The rest of you can do as you please."

"As you wish, Sire," came the response.

A few minutes later, the pundit was announced to the court. More than half the court had left already. Most of those who stayed were waiting for a quick laugh, some were hoping for a battle of wits. There were a few who stayed in the hope of seeing Birbal finally being outwitted. Birbal was as much loved as he was envied, for being Emperor Akbar's favourite minister.

The pundit looked like he was an extremely learned man. He wore a red headdress, walked in confidently and bowed before Emperor Akbar.

"Jahanpanah," he said. "I have come all the way from Madurai. I have but one wish in Agra. I wanted an audience with you. And I am ever so grateful to you for allowing me this privilege. You see, I am considered the smartest man in all of Madurai. However, so many travellers have told me about the great wit that Birbal displays. I wanted to experience this for myself."

Emperor Akbar looked puzzled. "What is it, Punditji? What are you asking for?"

"Sire, I want to test my knowledge and understanding of the world against this gem of your court. Against Birbal, if I may," replied the pundit. He looked tense as he waited for Emperor Akbar's reply.

"Birbal, come here," Akbar beckoned to his minister. He leaned over from his throne and whispered to Birbal. "I am very tired, Birbal. And very hungry too. This is not the time for one of your long-winded adventures. Please get this conversation over quickly. Time is of the essence here."

Turning to the pundit, Emperor Akbar said, "Please go ahead, learned Sir. It is an honour to entertain a pundit of your calibre in my court."

"Ah, Jahanpanah, this is not entertainment. This is a test of all things wit," came the reply. He bowed low. But his joy and relief at his request being granted were clear.

He turned towards Birbal, straightened his back, held his head high and said, "Tell me, Birbal, do you want to answer a hundred easy questions, or one very difficult one?"

"Well, Sir, we have all had a long day at court," said Birbal. "Everyone here is tired. I know you are to return to Madurai tomorrow. Your journey may be long and arduous, I am sure. Why don't we settle for one really difficult question for this evening?"

"As you wish, Sir," said the pundit, with a small smile on his face. "My one question is – What came first, the chicken or the egg?"

"Why, that's easy, Punditji," came Birbal's answer. "The chicken, of course," he added, with a smile on his face.

"The chicken!" exclaimed the pundit as all the courtiers leaned in. The low mutterings among the courtiers seemed to grow louder with each passing second.

"He's got him!"

"How is Birbal going to justify this answer?"

"This pundit is going to be the downfall of Birbal!"

"I think he's found his match here!"

"Even the emperor looks confused!"

Whispers floated around the room, seeming to gather momentum with each passing moment. The hum of voices grew louder.

Emperor Akbar raised his hand. "Silence!" he commanded. He motioned to the pundit. "Punditji, are you satisfied?"

The pundit bowed his head at Emperor Akbar.

Then, with a small, sly smile on his face, he turned towards Birbal and said, "The chicken? How can you explain that, Sir?"

"Ah!" said Birbal, twirling his moustache. "Punditji, I am afraid this is your second question! Our terms were, one question from you and one answer from me. I am afraid the emperor is very tired now, Sir. With all due respect, Punditji, we must leave you now. Please allow us to retire."

And with that, Birbal moved his right arm gracefully and gently bowed to Emperor Akbar.

Emperor Akbar stood up from his throne and, with a twinkle in his eye, nodded his head towards the pundit and left the court.

The pundit stood, rooted to the spot, in shock, wonder and admiration. He had heard so much about Birbal's wit but now he had experienced it first-hand.

The stories in this collection are adapted from the following Amar Chitra Katha comics:

Birbal the Genius

HOW AKBAR MET BIRBAL
Script: Dev Nadkarni
Art: Ram Waeerkar

THE CORRUPT OFFICIAL
Script: Dev Nadkarni
Art: Ram Waeerkar

THE WISE ANSWER
Script: Dev Nadkarni
Art: Ram Waeerkar

Gopal the Jester

GOPAL IN THE SWEET SHOP
Script: Urmila Sinha
Art: Souren Roy

GOPAL AND THE THIEF
Script: Urmila Sinha
Art: Souren Roy

Raman the Matchless Wit

RAMAN THE MATCHLESS WIT
Script: Subba Rao
Art: Ram Waeerkar

Raman of Tenali

RAMAN OF TENALI
Script: Kamala Chandrakant
Art: Ram Waeerkar

THE AMAR CHITRA KATHA CHAPTER BOOK SERIES

India's rich tapestry is woven together by her stories. These tales can be from the great epics and mythology, or from the ancient history of this rich land. But sometimes the stories of the people, passed down from generation to generation – told at bedtimes and celebrations, in schools and homes – are the most astounding. These are the stories that are part of the great collective inheritance from our past generations.

The Amar Chitra Katha chapter book series brings together some of the greatest tales in the Amar Chitra Katha catalogue. These stories are a celebration of the great collective inheritance from our past generations and aim to bring the reader closer to the thoughts and traditions that make up our country's identity.

The first set in the series, Amar Chitra Katha Folktales Collection, includes *Buddhist Stories*, *Tales of Wit and Wisdom* and *Funny Folktales*.

The second set in the series, Timeless Classics From Amar Chitra Katha, includes *Amazing Folktales*, *Fascinating Stories* and *Unusual Fables*.

The third set in the series, Most Loved Amar Chitra Katha Stories, includes *Jataka Tales*, *Fabulous Fables from India* and *Witty Minister Stories*.

 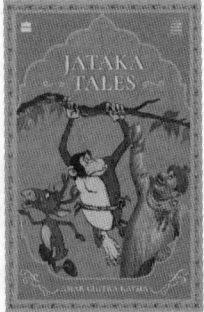 

ABOUT ACK

Amar Chitra Katha was founded in 1967 and is a household name in India. It is synonymous with the visual reinvention of the quintessentially Indian stories from the great epics, mythology, history, literature, oral folktales and many other sources.

With a heavy bent on authenticity and meticulous research, Amar Chitra Katha prides itself on being the most informative and trusted storyteller for children. The stories in this series have been adapted directly from the comics for young readers.

Today, Amar Chitra Katha is a cultural phenomenon, custodian of more than 400 comics in 20+ languages that have sold 100+ million copies to date. Amar Chitra Katha is available in bookstores, online and across digital platforms.